THE POETRY OF SPORT
and
THE SPORT OF POETRY

FRANK BARONE

eFrog Press, 2020

For Charlie, my grandson, who plays sports
and has fun playing with words.

INTRODUCTION

Sport can be fun. Sport can be exhilarating. Sport can be exhausting. But can it be poetic? Enjoy these poems and watch words, phrases, and metaphors leap from the page into the streets where we "swatted all those pink Spaldeens from sewer cover to sewer cover;" onto the court where the "ball [took] flight from . . . fingertips . . . [and] arced up and down into the hoop;" onto the green as Charlie's putt "crawled toward the slope then rolled down and down and down to curve gently and drop accurately into the center of the hole."

Play it in reverse. Can poetry mimic sport? The reader will enjoy the contest exhibited in these poems, as every word works with a teammate to form a lyrical phrase, and every phrase competes for metaphoric honors. Yes, poetry can mimic sport.

Barone's love of poetry and his gift in creating it is only too evident in these pages. The reader should take his time and sip each line like he might sip from a glass of fine wine.

C. Johnson

CONTENTS

LET'S PLAY POETRY

I come here without a Frisbee for you to toss
or ball and gloves to play catch.
Don't have a basketball to dribble and shoot hoops
or a soccer ball to kick around into a net.
But I do have some words for you to play with.
If you'll just look closely
and take time to reread this poem
you will find lines filled with objects called nouns
and action words known as verbs.
Toss a few of these words onto a piece of paper
or choose some you can find in your journal
and start to practice with them
until they begin to work together as a team
move with rhythm across the page.
And if you can see or hear a metaphor
as it surprises you in its flight toward your imagination,
grab it, jump high, and slam-dunk its message
about beauty or joy or love of writing poetry
this game we play for fun with our friends.

ABOUT MYSELF

I am a purple balloon
filled with metaphors and dreams
a hummingbird searching for hope in every flower
a green fairway waiting with open arms
for you to visit.
I am the books you read
that show you the stories of my life
the Number 2 yellow pencil I use
whenever my imagination prompts me
to create pictures with words.
I am the cup of cappuccino I order every day
to keep me company when I write.
I am this poem you hold in your hand and read
to keep my memory and our friendship alive.

STREETS AND SANDLOTS

Back then
we grew up on city streets
and neighborhood sandlots
those improvised fields
where we learned how to play our games
in spite of obstacles like parked cars
narrow boundaries and sewer drains
potholes and rock-filled infields.
We turned broom handles into bats
manhole covers into bases
and when we hit the cover off a baseball
we wrapped the sphere of string in tape
and kept on playing.
We made the rules
supervised ourselves
and needed no parental pressure
no adult involvement
to choose up sides and have fun growing up.
Then, years later, Little League came along
and gave every kid a chance to play in uniforms
on manicured fields
in front of grandstands filled with parents.
Looking back,
I'm grateful for the creativity and independence I learned
on those narrow city streets and rocky neighborhood sandlots.
Even now, I can look at a broom handle
and see a young lad taking his swings,
and my imagination can turn open fields
into baseball diamonds
where youngsters still race against the wind
to catch their dreams.

THESE ELDERLY ATHLETES

I admire these elderly athletes
who rise early in the morning
to arrive at the local golf course
eager to loosen their muscles
groove their swings on the driving range
sharpen their putting strokes
greet their partners
and get ready to play the game of their life
by driving the ball off the first tee
down the middle of the fairway
in spite of arthritic hands and aching backs,
knee operations, hip replacements,
and other age-related handicaps.
These elderly athletes continue to display
respect for the game, a passion to perform,
a competitive spirit, and a sense of humor
to offset any mis-hits or wayward shots.
No matter our age
we play this sport for fun.
It also helps to keep us young.

ODE TO OLDER PEOPLE

The 87-year-old regular at the coffee shop
entertains us with his stories
about Chicago gangsters and politicians.
My 91-year-old cousin
can step out onto a dance floor
and not embarrass herself or her partner.
My 86-year-old golfing friend with her grooved swing
can still drive the ball a respectable distance down the fairway
and sink putts with consistent accuracy.
Even late in their careers
singers, comedians, actors, and writers
continue to satisfy my appetite for arts and entertainment
with memorable performances.
So with this poem
I celebrate the wonder and joy they pour into our lives
and for showing us how to hope and chase dreams
as we join this age group of older people.

TWICE BLESSED

Poets and other lovers
will always find beauty
in ordinary and common circumstances
even hidden in dark shadows
and dangerous situations.
The other day I saw beauty come up
from one of the troublesome hazards
on the golf course.
Among the rocks and reeds within the ditch
stood a blue heron.
As I approached my golf ball
some thirty yards short of the hazard
the heron stretched its wings
and almost without effort
began to lift its stately body
and fly off toward the trees
along the side of the fairway.
With this impressive sight in mind
I addressed my ball
swung the club
and watched my ball sail over the water
and land safely on the other side of the fairway.
Beauty may be found in the form of a blue heron
and in the flight of a well-hit golf ball.

ODE TO BASKETBALL

Oh, basketball
joy of my youth
delightful orb of park
and schoolyard playground
how I loved to dribble you
on concrete court or wooden floor
and bounce you up against the backboard
or swish you through netted rims.
I thrilled to pass you off
to cutting teammates on fast breaks
or steal you with quick thrust of hand
and quicker feet
then run and gun
and run some more
for sheer joy of running.
Oh, basketball
even now I feel you on my fingertips
cradled in my hands
feet off the ground
arms extended above my head
released in an arc of rainbow
toward the basket
like a poem in flight
you and I never to descend
but always suspended in air
in hope
in glory
filled with promise
and forever young.

BASKETBALL BALLET

Watch the playmaker
race down court
fake left
dribble right
pass the ball
almost without looking
behind his back
to the open teammate
in the middle
who glides around his man
slides inside
turns
rises on his toes
leaps
spins
and extends his hand
over his head
above the rim
and thrusts the ball
down
into the basket
for an easy
wham
jam
two-point slam
dunk.

OUR NATIONAL PASTIME

The baseball season has come again
with a celebration of flags and anthems
parades of players
crowds of fans
the introduction of lineups
and the ceremonial first pitch
by a distinguished someone or other.
In more informal settings
baseball begins whenever
dads and moms and sons and daughters
play catch in backyards
or kids swing a bat and chase a ball on playgrounds.
But recently our national pastime
has given way to a more popular sport
not played on grassy fields between foul lines.
Our modern youth now spends more time
with games played between the space of their thumbs
on any electronic device they can get their hands on.
The crack of the bat has given way
to the click of a button
and while I applaud the skill and intensity needed
for this new sport
I will always be grateful for the lessons learned
the friends made
and the maturity I gained with my teammates
as we swung a bat and chased a ball
on green fields between foul lines.

LITTLE WHITE BALL

On the golf course
I follow the little white ball
from trapped fairway to neatly trimmed green
until it hides in the cup
giggling like a playful child.

LET'S PLAY A GAME

Let's play a game.
Let's grab a handful of words we can find
stored on the top shelves of closets
or those words scattered like socks under beds
stuffed animals lying around the room
or hiding behind chairs.
Don't spend too much time searching for fancy words.
Ordinary, well-used words will work just fine
like the leaves we see along our streets
the boxes of cereal in our supermarkets
shoes in department stores
swings in playgrounds
drawings and pictures on the walls of classrooms
and the rows of books in libraries.
Books contain a great treasure of words we can use
to play our game.
Just look along the lines as you read
for nouns that surprise your eyes
verbs that punch you in the stomach
or whisper in your ear
and metaphors that show you different ways
of looking at a cloud or a purple balloon.
You can even find some words in the songs you sing
and in the rhythm of the music you hear.
Now spread your handful of words onto the page
and begin to select and shape them into a bridge
that will reach out from your imagination
to touch the hearts of others.
In this game we play everyone wins,
readers as well as writers.
And, as in every game,
remember to have some fun.

LITTLE LEAGUE PRACTICE

Way to go, Coach.
You show those nine-year-old Little Leaguers
how to throw and catch,
swing the bat, field positions,
back up the play at every base,
hit the cut-off man, and other nuances of the game.
Make them practice these skills
over and over until they get them right
over and over until they perform without physical or mental error.
Penalize them by making them run laps
over and over when they mess up.
When they mess up, use your big coach's voice
to let them know they will have to do it better next time
and every time if they want to play on your team.
I know you also encourage good play
yet I can hear your big coach's voice
when you single out players for shoddy performance.
Nine-year-old Little Leaguers will have their ups and downs
so don't turn them off to this sport.
Remember, Coach, this game involves more than mechanics.
Teach them team play and respect for themselves.
Help them to form friendships.
Show them how to win, but also how to accept losing.
The game should be fun, Coach.
Help them build upon good experiences
so they will feel enthusiastic about moving up to the next level
and be eager to improve upon the skills they have learned
as nine-year-old Little Leaguers.

"THE TEAM DEPENDS ON ME."
Nine-year-old Little Leaguer

Coaches train athletes to play the game
show them how to hit, field, and throw a baseball.
They encourage players to do their best
at every practice and in every game.
Patient coaches take performance beyond mechanics
teach teamwork and responsibility
the value of playing with enthusiasm
and for fun.

With his team trailing by two runs in the last inning
and with a three-ball, two-strike count
this nine-year-old Little Leaguer felt the pressure
to come through in the clutch
especially after his coach singled him out
in a pregame meeting with a negative comment
about his ability to hit the baseball.
With this one thought in mind, "The team depends on me,"
he swung his bat and connected with a solid smash
through the right side of the infield that scored a run.
As he stood on first base
he had another thought.
"I showed that coach I can get a clutch hit,
not for him, but for my teammates
who depend on me."
And he smiled.

FOR MY GOLFING PARTNER, C.J.

One bird in hand
may be worth more
than two in the bush
but the three birdies in a row
on the last three holes
of the back nine
at the local golf course
on October 22, 2018,
by my golfing partner, C.J.,
will remain a memorable experience
for both of us.

"OH BABY, BABY"

Jerry, one of my golfing friends,
has fun playing this sport
in spite of back pains
and other physical difficulties.
I admire the way he never complains
about his problems
and never will allow nasty words
to erupt from his mouth
after a poor swing or errant shot.
His positive attitude supports the idea
that golf should be fun
and backs it up with a sense of humor
and contagious laughter.
An excellent putter, he will often smile
to reinforce the pleasure at seeing his golf ball
drop into the cup
and begin to retrieve his ball
with a short, spontaneous strut
and with the hearty, tuneful phrase
"Oh Baby, Baby."

A FUN FOURSOME: FOR TAYLOR

Want to have a good game?
Then drive to the local golf course
and check in with Taylor at the clubhouse
and watch the way she signs you in
with a smile and friendly greetings.
Her smile and words will put you in the mood
to have some fun at the tees, no matter the distances,
along the fairways, in spite of the hazards,
and on the smooth greens with their slopes,
twists, turns, ups and downs.
Taylor makes my game special
because of her interest in and love of poetry.
At one of our recent meetings
when she asked for a copy of one of my poems
and I said, "Yes," she added with her ready smile
"May I give you a hug?"
My response, also with a smile,
came quickly and easily. "Sure."
She stepped around the counter
and we embraced with sincerity and gratitude
for our friendship.
Those feelings continue on the course
and help me to keep my drives straight
my fairway shots consistent
and my putts few and simple.
Golf, poetry, Taylor, and I make for a fun foursome.

MY BLUE BASEBALL HAT

I grew up with "dem bums"
the loveable Dodgers of Brooklyn
listened to Red Barber call their games on radio
and when I could afford it
rode the trolley and then the el to Ebbets Field
that green Garden of Eden surrounded by city streets
to watch Dolph Camilli dance around first base
Cookie Lavagetto cover the hot corner
Roy Campanella crouch behind the plate
Preacher Roe toss strikes on the mound
Duke Snider race to the wall in center
Ducky Medwick patrol left field
and Carl Furillo throw out runners with his rifle arm
in front of the short fence in right.
My hero, Pee Wee Reese,
handled shortstop with poise and intelligence
helped Jackie Robinson succeed at second base
and eased Jackie's tortured introduction into the Big Leagues.
These and other players on this team
taught me to play the game with head and heart
as well as with bat and glove.
From them I learned about teamwork and friendship
to think quickly and creatively
accept challenges, push past or around obstacles,
and to play the game and any sport just for fun.
To this day I still wear my blue baseball hat
with its distinct white "B" for Brooklyn
with pride, loyalty, and grateful memories.

"IF A TREE FALLS…"

This tree did not fall in the forest
but on the golf course as I searched for my ball
in the short rough next to the tree-lined fairway.
While my eyes scanned the ground
some loud sounds surprised my ears
sounds as loud as gunshots
or the blade of a heavy axe smacked against a log.
Alerted, I looked around
to discover the source of my worry
found nothing
then saw my golf ball
hit it back into the fairway
scrambled into my cart
and removed myself from possible danger.
Just then, about forty yards behind me,
a tree crashed to the ground.
Grateful to have escaped unharmed
I continued with my game
along with the echo of that fallen tree
to remind me to hit my golf ball
in the middle of the fairway
away from such unforeseen hazards.

A HITTING MACHINE

His eyes locked onto the pitch
followed its path toward the plate
saw it approach the strike zone
and told his mind to tell his hands
to unload and make a level swing with the bat
and smash the ball.
That day, March 18, at practice,
Charlie hit pitch after pitch after pitch
ten straight drives past or over the infielders
into the outfield
and heard Coach Mark call out to him,
"Charlie, you're a hitting machine."
At his game the next day
Charlie stood comfortable and confident
in the batter's box
and continued his progress
in hand-eye coordination
with three more solid hits.
Keep on making progress, Charlie,
with sure-handed glove work
strong accurate throws
smart base running
and hit after hit after hit.

SURPRISE ME

Surprise me.
Write words that fill my eyes with pictures.
Try to grab a star and hang it on one of your blue lines
or sprinkle your poem with dew drops
that sparkle in morning's sunlight.
Let me hear waves laughing
as they race to meet at the sandy shore
or help me hear those whispers from the wings
of a busy hummingbird.
Place an Oreo cookie in between a couple of metaphors
or press a piece of dark chocolate
inside a simile to excite my taste buds.
Surround your poem with the fragrance of lilacs
the aroma of a cup of cappuccino
or the scent of tomato sauce
on top of a plate of spaghetti
or decorating a slice of eager-to-be-eaten pizza.
Surprise me with words that alert my senses
wake up my imagination
touch my heart
make me laugh or cry
words that could strike a blow to my stomach
words that will help me to remember your name
and the fun we will have
when we come together to write and read our poems.

THE POETRY CAFÉ

Let's treat ourselves today
to lunch at the Poetry Café.
We can start by sampling
a platter of poetic appetizers
featuring succulent cinquains
tasty tankas, seasoned haiku
and lusty limericks.
Or we may select a salad of free verse
to limber up our taste buds.
For our entree we may choose
a steak of epic proportions
a kebab of odes
the country-fried pastoral
or a narrative casserole.
All entrees come with side orders
of iambs and dactyls.
To help us enjoy our meal
we can sip from a glass
of well-aged Shakespearean sonnets.
And for dessert we'll celebrate this time
with couplet cookies soaked in metered rhyme.

THREE YOUNG BUCKS

On the fifteenth tee
we watched a threesome in front of us
come leaping up in single file
from the riverbank
dash and bound across the fairway
then disappear into the trees beyond.
They had no clubs or golf bags
to slow themselves down.
Golf had no interest for them.
They had come across the course
to play in the river
and now, refreshed, they headed back
along a familiar trail
to their home in the hills.

THIS GOLFING MEMORY

My thirteen-year-old grandson, Charlie,
our golfing companion, C.J., and I
all had fun on the golf course yesterday.
Golf provided us with the scenario
to build some pleasant memories.
With his knowledge as a teacher,
scholar, world traveler, and student of human nature,
C.J. helped to create some of those memories.
He personally instructed Charlie
on the courtesy and etiquette
we all observe from tee to green
and made it easier for Charlie to smile
and not give up hope after missed or errant shots.
When Charlie pitched a wedge onto the first green
C.J. and I shouted approval.
And when Charlie smashed a drive 150 yards
high and straight down the fairway
we both laughed, hooted, and howled
at the perfection of this performance.
Then, when Charlie's approach shot landed
at the back of a down-sloping green
C.J. spoke to him about the appropriate speed
for his putt to reach the hole
while I stood at the flag about fifty feet away
and indicated the probable line of flight.
After Charlie stroked the putt
we watched as it crawled toward the slope
then rolled down and down and down
to curve gently and drop accurately
into the center of the hole.
For this first time on the local golf course

and his only putt on the fifth hole
we celebrated this golfing memory
with well-deserved high-fives and fist bumps
and honored Charlie for his "Putt of the Year."

CIVILIZED SPORT

I call golf a cultured, civilized sport
a game played by gentle men
and gentle ladies
who enjoy the aesthetics of their environment
respect the course with its rough
and all its bunkers, traps, trees, water hazards,
and hard-to-read, difficult-to-putt greens.
I applaud all golfers
who play by the rules
accept penalties with grace
replace their divots
repair their ball marks
and rake the sand.
Such golfers maintain a steady pace of play
and neither lag behind
nor push their shots ahead
to crowd the foursome in front of them.
I admire these sporting individuals
who play the game for fun
and who can laugh when they mis-hit
instead of blaming the club, the ball,
the poor lie,
then curse whatever local golf gods
may have witnessed their ill fortune.
Give me a starting time
with any of these gentle men
or gentle ladies
and I will enjoy a pleasant round of golf
no matter what my score.

A GAME OF TAG

I am waiting for the words
to stop playing hide-and-seek with me
waiting for them to come out
from behind whatever tree they are hiding
whatever hole they have crawled into.
I want the words to jump out
and show me their faces
run across the empty space between us
and leap, laughing and screaming,
into my arms
then tumble onto the page
and shout, "We're home.
Tag. You're it."

STICKBALL

Where does hand-eye coordination come from?
Maybe from the thin handle of a broomstick
when we played ball in the streets
and swatted all those pink Spaldeens
from sewer cover to sewer cover
or hit the fuzz off tennis balls in the handball courts
or at the schoolyard.
Learning and coordination come fast
when the eye must be trained to watch the ball bounce
and then meet it with a smooth swing and roll of the wrists
to make contact so that ball and bat converge at the moment of
truth
and the Spaldeen flattens then rockets away
in a line drive past the fielders
or in a graceful arc beyond the point of no return.
Back then we didn't call it hand-eye coordination.
In our youth we only played for the love of the game
and because our young bodies needed to run,
throw, catch, hit, and sometimes even hook slide on cement
into a base or home plate.
Most of all we played for fun and camaraderie
long before we knew what that word meant.
Today's youngsters have different games they play
but I'm not sure they have as much fun as we did
with just the handle of a broomstick and a pink ball
on city streets.

STICKBALL: A PROSE POEM

Where does hand-eye coordination come from? Maybe early on from games of marbles, jacks, and pick-up-sticks, boxball or stoopball, from spinning tops on the sidewalk, or pulling a yo-yo on a string up and down, sideways, and around the world.

But much could be said for later on when we played stickball in the street where we swatted all those pink Spaldeens with the thin handle of a cut-off broomstick from sewer to sewer, or smashed them against the wall at the handball courts, or drove them over the cyclone fence at the schoolyard. Learning and coordination come fast when the eye must be trained to watch the ball and then meet it with a smooth swing and a roll of the wrists to make contact so that the ball and the bat meet at the moment of truth and the Spaldeen flattens out then speeds away in a line drive past the fielders or flies up and away in a graceful arc beyond the point of no return.

Back then we didn't know about hand-eye coordination. In our youth we only played for the love of the game, because our young bodies needed to run, throw, hit, catch, and sometimes even slide on schoolyard cement into a base or home plate. Most of all, we played for fun and for the camaraderie that came from teamwork and from competing against our friendly opponents. When our games ended, we walked up to the corner candy shop to spend our few pennies for a soda and a chocolate bar, then headed home for dinner to regain our strength for the next day's athletic exhibitions.

We don't see games of stickball anymore. Kids now play video games. And while they may have great eye-thumb coordination, I wonder if they have as much fun growing up as we did.

SOME OF MY FAVORITE THINGS

Hummingbirds and lilacs
purple balloons and poetry
ice cream and dark chocolate
the game of golf and apricots
stories that invite my imagination
to explore possibilities
metaphors that surprise me
and songs that make me smile
the comfort of sunshine and sweaters
the ever-changing shapes of clouds
the presence of stars to dream upon
friends who listen and family members who care
the gift of hope.
These favorite things please my heart
and continue to help me celebrate
the joy and beauty waiting to greet me
each day of my life.

BIG GAME

There must be a high school basketball game on tonight
because the perky blond cheerleader
with her hair pulled back in a bouncy ponytail
enters the coffee shop with the required smile
dressed in her green-and-white cheerleader jacket
and long green sweatpants.
As part of her colorful outfit
she sports two male teenage admirers
one on each arm
and dangles them like trophies
in front of the crowd of afternoon coffee drinkers
while she goes over her routines
and practices her moves
for tonight's big game.

OUTSIDE THE FOUL LINES: FOR GREG

I never bought into the cliché
that catchers wear the "tools of ignorance."
It takes brains and guts
talent and tact
to take command of the entire field
while squatting behind the plate
outside the foul lines.
Catchers must calm those pitchers
who hit a batter with a fastball
and settle them down
when they load the bases with walks
give up a line drive or a scratch hit
past the infield
or the pop fly beyond the reach of his outfielders.
Catchers must be intelligent
to set up hitters with the correct pitches
alert to fire the ball with a strong accurate arm
on attempted steals
and quick to field the well-placed bunt
or glove the foul ball headed toward the stands.
They serve as the last wall of defense
when they guard the plate against the runner
who rounds third at full speed
in a dash to score with a hook slide
or a body slam to dislodge the ball
from the catcher's grip.
His teammates and manager
his fans and even his opponents
respect the men who command the entire field
and squat down behind the plate
outside the foul lines.

THE 19TH HOLE

Golfers know the 19th hole as a "watering" place
where they can settle in with their buddies
partake of their favorite beverages
and unwind after chasing the golf ball
down the fairway onto the green
and into the cup for 18 holes.
After a round I prefer to drive away from the links
toward the local coffee shop
for a cappuccino
talk with friends
read a book
and when the creative opportunity presents itself
do a little writing.
This comfortable environment
with its appealing atmosphere and a tasty cappuccino
always cheers me up
renews my strength
and prepares me
for my next pleasant excursion on the golf course
chasing the ball down the fairway
onto the green and into the cup
no matter how many strokes it may take.

WHY WE PLAY THE GAME

It does not matter which golf course we play.
It could be the challenging championship courses
or the shorter but demanding executive layout
because aside from the drives off the tee
the long shots from the fairway
the delicate chips from up close on the fringe
and the putts on the green
we also play golf for the sunshine
the fresh air and the exercise
the aesthetics of the peaceful glen
sheltered by the silent hills
and especially for the conversation and laughter
between friends who enjoy each other's presence
and the respect they show for the game.

PLAYING IN THE DIRT

Poets like to get their hands dirty
to find metaphors in mud pies
and to finger-paint their dreams
with all the colors of the rainbow.
They like to shove their hands
deep into the dirt to plant words,
work the soil, then watch those words
blossom into poems.
Poets don't mind looking through dusty attics
or cleaning out the garage
in their search for objects they can polish
and present to their readers
through clear and memorable pictures.
Nor do poets mind the messy, necessary rough drafts
where they erase words, change phrases,
tighten or rearrange lines
until their poems read smoothly
and flow with easy rhythm
without any trace of dirt or dust
to disturb the harmony between writer and reader.
Their work done
poets will wash their hands
so they will show no evidence of all the fun they've had
while playing in the dirt.

OUT OF BOUNDS

Done with her shopping
a woman enters the back nine of the golf course
from the nearby street
and walks close to the tree-lined, out-of-bounds markers
along the right side of the fairway.
She knows exactly which dense
low-hanging leaves
to push aside
and descend to the edge of the hidden riverbed
at the camp of her homeless buddies
to bring them the food she brought
and help them survive
for another day.

PLAYING WITH LANGUAGE

Call it what you will
a bit of, "Now you see it, now you don't" chicanery
a card sharp's sleight of hand
or deceptive manipulation by a nimble-fingered juggler.
Those with somewhat larger vocabularies
would name it a case of legerdemain
or prestidigitation
a crafty magician's artful machination.
The sports-minded would say
it looks like the old flea-flicker
the hidden ball trick
a feint, a dodge on the basketball court
or some shifty maneuver on the football field
to hoodwink the opposition into going one way
while the ball carrier scampers in the other direction.
Nonbelievers would label it a sham, a bluff,
a fabrication, a ruse,
some subterfuge or form of hocus-pocus
to baffle less perceptive observers.
But I have heard this word spoken by my daughter
who heard it from her brother
who heard it from a client.
And now, more recently, I have heard it twice on TV
that most trustworthy and reliable source
of up-to-the-minute information
delivered by respected reporters
who called it nothing more or less
than pure, new-fashioned
"trickeration."
And that, dear reader,
shows us how, through the playful invention of new words,
language grows and enriches our lives.

OUR CADDIE

The caddie for our foursome
suggested the proper clubs for us to swing
gave us correct yardage on our approaches
and indicated the preferred targets to aim for
down the fairway.
On the greens his knowledge of slopes and speeds
resulted in putts that rolled close to the hole
and even dropped in to save us some strokes.
He also took time to snap a few pictures
to record our presence at this fabled golf course.
And when we faced difficult shots
he reduced our tension with well-timed humor.
But our caddie has another job
as a single parent taking care of his young son.
Not an easy task.
Though after observing his respect for this course
his knowledge of angles and approaches
and how to avoid or recover from hazards
his patience in handling varied personalities
and his use of humor to diffuse tense situations
I have reason to believe he will lead his son successfully
down life's fairways.

GAME PLAN

A coffee shop can be the neutral site
where two disgruntled mothers
meet with the glib team coach
to listen to him explain away
any perceived injustice done to their sons.
And while I overhear his blather of clichés
and predictable offensive and defensive arguments
it becomes apparent he has used this game plan before
on other concerned and offended parents
and more than likely
and still more unfortunately
he will use it again and again
and so continue to add to his winning record.

A GAME OF CATCH

Fathers need to play catch with their sons
more often.
Same goes for fathers and daughters.
Nothing wrong in tossing a ball
back and forth
to establish a connection through play
and create some memories for later in life.
Even when sons and daughters grow older
fathers should not abandon their children
to video screens and battery-operated plastic forms
of self-entertainment.
If only on special occasions
like birthdays or Father's Day
or the Fourth of July
fathers should resurrect the old ball and glove
loosen up their arms
and reconnect with sons and daughters
through a game of catch.
It will take just a few tosses
or perhaps a few years
for the children to recall these times
as unspoken acts of love
an exchange of gifts between fathers and children
with every toss and catch
catch and toss . . . and catch.

BASKETBALL MEMORIES
PASSED OFF TO MY GRANDSON

I still remember how to play basketball
how to catch the ball on the fingers
and let it settle into the soft palm of my hand
how to make a bounce pass or a chest pass
while looking at the defender and not at a teammate.
I still remember it took me a long time
to gain the proper form and the correct technique
to shoot the basketball with elbows in
and arms extended to allow the ball to roll off the fingertips
with just enough arc and spin to reach the front of the rim
and drop through the net
or to place the ball gently against the backboard
for it to angle down through the hoop.
It took a while to learn how to dribble equally well with either
hand
left or right
to keep my head up and not look at the ball
as I drove against the opponent and toward the basket
while making quick decisions about how to feint him out of his
socks
and continue the drive toward the rim
or fake the layup and pass off
to a quick-closing teammate across the lane
knowing that a good pass meant as much as a good shot.
I still remember the speed and delight of a well-planned fast
break
and then turning to race back down court to play defense
pressure the ball
reach in or lay back for a steal
or set up to play position against an opponent

to deny him a pass or block him out for the rebound.
What do I remember about playing basketball?
The fun I had.
The friends I made.
The confidence I gained.
The respect I won.
I learned how to make quick decisions
to cooperate with and rely on other players for the good of the
team.
Did it involve hard work?
Sure it did.
Hours of practice. Buckets of sweat.
Frequent pain. Often injuries.
Basketball helped me develop a skill
and the discipline I could use later in life.
After all these years I can no longer play the game
but basketball memories continue to give me smiles.
I can still picture the ball taking flight from my fingertips
see it arc up and down into the hoop
and I can still hear the ball swish through the nets.
After all these years
I am still smiling.

BASKETBALL SHOES

Dig deep into the closet
then search far under the bed
until your hand closes on
those ten-year-old, high-top basketball shoes
and your eyes light up with memories
of full-court contests and half-court pick-up games
of two-on-two, three-on-three,
"horse," and "around-the-world"
and those countless hours practicing
layups, set shots, jump shots, foul shots,
fast breaks, no-look and behind-the-back passes,
the dribble with either hand,
the pick-and-roll,
blocking out, setting screens
and leaping for rebounds.
Now wipe the dust from those shoes
and, one by one,
slip your feet into their cushioned insides
tie the laces tight
and see if your feet remember
how to fake left and right
cut and pivot
accelerate to top speed with the first step
and squeak to a stop within inches of committing a foul
before you pass the ball to a teammate
or lift straight up for a jump shot
or fly toward the basket to place the ball against the backboard
and into the net.
Try to forget the sprained fingers
twisted ankles
pulled hamstrings

charley horses
bruised ribs
and sore knees.
They never mattered nor slowed your steps
as you raced up and down the court
young and free
young and without fear or worry
young and laughing at every challenge
young and enjoying the camaraderie of teammates
and even now
ten or twenty or fifty years later
still young at heart
still grateful for all the memories
rediscovered in a pair of high-top basketball shoes.

HAVE FUN WITH WORDS

Follow Alice through the looking glass
into a wonderland of words and wild adventures.
Sail with words toward tropical islands
and ride off with words toward enchanted castles.
Search for words in dictionaries
within the pages of a thesaurus
or inside the chapters of any good story.
Smile or laugh when the words of a poem
surprise your eyes and your imagination.
Hold hands with words when they lead you
into mysterious caves and through magical kingdoms.
Fling a fistful of words into the evening sky
and watch them turn into stars.
Slip a few nouns into your piggy bank every once in a while
and always carry a couple of verbs in your pocket
in case of an emergency.
Sprinkle some metaphors on your cereal for breakfast
and, after supper, treat yourself
to some chocolate-covered metaphors for dessert.
Remember to wash your hands frequently with soap and words.
When you find some new words that you like
hang them up in the closet
so you can wear them on special occasions.
When you go to bed at night
put one or two of your favorite words under the pillow
so you will have pleasant dreams.
But, most of all, sing and dance and have fun with words.
Words like it when you play with them.
Sometimes, if you listen quietly,
you can hear them chuckle and giggle.

METAPHORS IN MOTION

So, you want to write a poem.
Put on some music
and let your ears listen to the beat
to the rhythm and the way the instruments
sing to each other.
Poetry moves with rhythm from line to line
in harmony with words that hold each other lightly
and glide and flow and dance across the page.
When you feel the beat
give your feet permission to tap and slide
and bounce from side to side
and use your eyes to watch the way
your fingers, elbows, shoulders, and hips
enjoy blending in with the music.
Now loosen the strings that bind your imagination
so it can jump up and hop onto the dance floor
and create its own moves
its own metaphors in motion.
Then, as the music comes to a satisfying conclusion,
let your imagination preserve this moment
in a word picture
to show the world how much fun it can be
to dance with words and write a poem.

WHAT BASKETBALL HAS TAUGHT ME

This game I still love
has taught me to think creatively
improvise on the run
process information quickly
and make rapid decisions.
This game has taught me
the patience to practice a variety of moves
to challenge those bigger and perhaps more talented
than myself
and to even the odds by using my head to outwit challengers
and my feet to speed past defenders.
From this game I have learned
to recognize the skills of teammates
and open up opportunities for them to compete and succeed.
This sport I still love
has taught me to play the game for fun
for the exhilaration and satisfaction
of performing well no matter how difficult the contest
and no matter what the outcome
to be gracious in victory
and learn from defeat.
Even more, this game has taught me
to always keep my head up
and my eyes fixed on the goal.

WHAT SHOULD WE PUT INTO A POEM?

What should we put into a poem?
Something up in the sky that catches the eye
like a cloud or a star
the moon or the tail of a comet
but also whatever we discover close to us
that asks for our attention
like the smile on the child holding a purple balloon
or the sign held by the homeless man on the street corner.
We'll put some words into our poem
that can splash in the surf
or zoom around a racetrack
words with pictures inside them
of sunsets and lonely country roads
and city sidewalks turned into playgrounds.
There will be room in our poem for giggles
a bit of nonsense and some silly laughter
and perhaps even the beginning of a teardrop.
Our poem may also include a daydream
a sprinkle of magic dust
a couple of surprises
and just a hint of mystery.
We'll make sure the words we choose
move along their lines with ease and rhythm.
When we come to the end of our poem
we'll try to see to it that the last few lines
encourage our readers to read it again
just for the fun of it
or because our poem has awakened old memories
or opened some windows to refresh our sleepy imaginations.
Playful imaginations can be good friends.
They may even save our lives.

TO PLAY IN THE SUNSHINE

What sounds do you hear in the silence
and what do you see with your eyes closed?
And when you permit your imagination
to escape from its dark room
and run outside to play in the sunshine
does it chase shadows and butterflies
sing in harmony with the wind
jump into puddles of ideas
splash in a river of metaphors
and gather words like autumn leaves?
When day turns toward evening
does your imagination ever look up
to talk with the stars and dance with the moon
then come home just before bedtime
to tell you stories about the people it met
who bared their bruised hearts and secret scars
before it falls asleep
with dreams about all the caves and castles
it can explore tomorrow?

PRACTICE SESSION

In the early afternoon
when the rain eased off
the teenage girl steps out of her house
bounces her basketball on her damp driveway
and dribbles toward the freestanding hoop
for a slick layup
then dribbles back to a pretend foul line
for a graceful jump shot.
And while gray clouds threaten more rain
she continues to practice her moves
dribbling left and right past imaginary defenders
for creative baskets
and shooting long two-pointers from different angles.
Then, as if to support and encourage her practice session
the sun pierces through the clouds
and the two of us, the sun and I,
smile at this future all-star.

POETRY CAN DO THAT

Teachers and writers always tell us,
"Write what you know."
Good advice, of course.
But I would add a few more categories
to help young poets find the words
to fill the blank pages of their writing journals
so the lines will crawl with ideas
show pictures, paint scenes,
and sparkle with surprise and wonder.
Young poets can write not only about eye-catching sights
like a sunrise or sunset
but also poems about a child's tears
teenage loneliness
skinned knees and bruised feelings
the rage of rebellion
the loss of friends and scars from abuse.
They can write poems as big as a mountain
or as small as a spider
as wide as the horizon
or as skinny as the string on a kite
poems as scary as a monster
or as gentle as a whisper.
I would also suggest that young poets
can write about what they don't know
as a way to make sense of the world around them
or to understand what they may find hard to accept.
Writing can do that.
It can help us to sort through mixed feelings
or to bring some order out of chaos
and harmony from the madness surrounding our lives.
Most of all, writing can be a pleasurable activity

a challenge to play with words
and at the same time struggle with them
until all the lines, shapes, colors,
figures, actions, and emotions come together
to complete this creative act born of love
and of the desire to share that love with others.
Poets can do that.
They create, then share their art
so we may see this world and ourselves more clearly.
Poetry allows us to slide open the window of our imagination
to see the beauty of metaphor
hear the cadence and rhythm of language
and to breathe in the fresh air of hope.
Poetry can do that, and more.

OUR FAVORITE BASKETBALL PLAYER

Good morning, basketball fans.
Welcome to the Allied Gardens Rec Center
for the second game on this rainy Saturday
between the Green Giants and their Purple Lightning opponents.
The Green Giants have shown steady improvement
in their dribbling, passing, aggressive defense
and accurate shooting.
This day, February 6th,
would see another of their players
score his first basket
on a shot from the right side of the court
that swished through the net
and when it did
his dad, his mom, his uncle, and I
shouted, smiled, laughed, applauded
and jumped with happiness
for Number 22, Charlie Baird,
our favorite basketball player.

MARCH MADNESS

The young boy's grandfather
stands close to the basketball hoop
in the driveway
and watches his grandson practice his moves.
When the ball bounces his way
he scoops it up and shows the future star
how to let fly a soft high hook shot
that floats and arcs down and through the nets
while with his other hand
he supports his body with his cane.

KEEP MOVING

Do a dance.
Swing your arms.
Sway your hips and shake your legs.
Impromptu steps
on makeshift dance floors
in make-believe ballrooms
will do nicely to warm up the blood
keep it flowing into those arthritic fingers and hands
loosen those stiff spines and creaky knees
and lift some of the weight from your shoulders.
Don't be embarrassed
and don't worry about looking like a fool.
Dancing will help you to smile more
bring some color to your face
and lengthen your life span.
Besides, it can be great fun
especially if you sing along with the music.

NO DEFENSE

The poem falls
soft as a snowflake
upon the tongue
then tingles there
for less than a moment
before it dissolves like manna
to satisfy our hunger for Beauty.
The poem lands
gentle as a petal
in the palm of the imagination
diffuses its fragrance
and awakens our desire for Beauty.
But sometimes the poem bursts before our eyes
in an unexpected explosion of words
that showers the senses with sharp metaphors
rips open our hearts
and leaves us wounded by Beauty.
Confronted by Her charms
She captivates our minds
and overwhelms our emotions.
We have no defense against Beauty.

DEFENSIVE GEMS

What better time than the last game of the season
for Charlie to show the progress he has made
as a fielder for the Orioles.
With bases loaded on a ball hit back to the mound
Charlie threw off his catcher's mask
stepped on home plate
and caught the ball thrown to him by the pitcher
for the force out.
Next batter, same play, same result,
another force at home
two back-to-back beauties
to get his team out of the inning
without giving up a run.
Then on the last play of the game
Charlie, now playing third, fielded a grounder
and whipped a strike to his second baseman
for the force on the runner coming from first.
Three defensive gems applauded by his teammates
his coach
and by all of his family and fans in the stands.

LIKE A CHAMPION

Even before this year's championship game began
I told my grandson, "Charlie, you already are a champion
because, win or lose, you always try your best."
And when the game began
he played like a champion
running up and down the court
to get in position to receive a pass
or defend against an opponent
diving into the pile to fight for loose basketballs
keeping his hands up to block shots
passing to open teammates
and shooting for the basket when he had the opportunity.
Charlie and his team finished in second place
but only champions like Charlie
get to play in the final game of the season.

MY POEM

My poem wears loose-fitting clothes
like a tee shirt and shorts
so it can breathe and move,
shimmy and shake,
rock and roll, bebop, doo-wop.
My poem has arms it can wave
to get your attention
and hands to squeeze your heart
grab your head and lift you off the ground.
My poem has legs to walk like a spider
or clomp like a ho-ho-ho giant.
My poem can race you around the world
or kick you in the shins.
My poem has feet to dance a waltz or a fox-trot
do the twist, the tango
mambo or samba
or even the hokey pokey.
My poem has a nose to help you smell the flowers
or yesterday's dumpster trash.
My poem has ears to hear you laugh
eyes to see your tears and smiles
and a mouth to sing the blues
or shout, "Watch out! The sky is falling."
My poem can whisper words that say,
"I like you. Be my friend."

WHAT POETRY DOES FOR ME

Poetry calms the tensions around my heart
quiets the doubts that wander through my mind
invites me to slow the pace of my life
listen to the music of words
and dance to their rhythms.
Poetry gives me the freedom to smile
when metaphors surprise my senses
challenges me to extend my vision
and explore new ways to show others
the neighborhoods where we work and play.
Poetry makes it easier for me
to introduce myself to strangers
and lets my friends know I think of them
every time I engage in the process of writing.
When they read my poems
I hope they will find some gift within the lines
that will recall memories or renew friendships.
Perhaps a metaphor will also surprise their senses
and give them the freedom to smile.

WHAT I CAN'T DO ANYMORE

I can't lead a fast break down the court
and pass the ball behind my back
to a driving teammate
or fake the defender to his left
and dribble around and up for two points
or leap to grab a rebound
or shoot a jump shot from beyond the circle.
I cannot bunt the ball down the line
and beat the throw to first
or steal another base
or race in from center field
to catch the short fly ball at my knees.
I can no longer run a half mile
or even just around the block.

WHAT I CAN STILL DO

I can still drive a golf ball a respectable distance
down the middle of the fairway.
I can still chip the ball close to the flag
and make my fair share of putts.
And I can also dream and hope
to read and write
and enjoy the arts and lunch with friends
savor a cup of cappuccino and remember Paris.
I can still smile with others
and laugh at myself.
My eyes can still grow wide and my heart warm
when I am surprised by unexpected gifts.
I am still startled by metaphors I have never heard
nor seen before.
I am still awed by beauty
and forever grateful for the presence of love in my life.

ODE TO NINETY

How do I feel on my ninetieth birthday?
Like my game has not finished
but moved into extra innings for a few more at bats
or into overtime with the basketball still in my hands
ready to dribble up court
eager for a shot at the hoop
or to pass off to a teammate for his winning score.
This game of life has helped me to improve
who I am and what I do.
Who am I? A parent who loves his children,
a grandfather grateful for the gift of his grandson,
a retired teacher who continues to love his students.
What do I do?
I read to enjoy the stories authors need to share with us
and the poetic language they use to express ideas
and reveal emotions.
I write to show others what I have seen and heard
and to describe my feelings about memories
or to capture the metaphors that surprise my senses.
I write to record the tragedy and comedy of daily life
to honor family and friendships
and the acts of people who care.
For as long as I can
I will enjoy my games of golf
my cups of cappuccino at my favorite coffee shop
and the fun and challenge of writing poems
in my nineties.

ABOUT THE AUTHOR

Frank Barone's three loves are family, sports, and poetry. In the current volume, Frank blends the three into a melodic whole. Growing up, Frank loved basketball, a love that continues in his poetry to this day. He also loved the form of baseball that was played on city streets with broom handles as bats, manhole covers as bases, and a quickly deteriorating "Spaldeen" with a pink rubber cover as the baseball.

The nun who first invited Frank to read poetry aloud in elementary school began his love of poetry. Even more, the metaphoric word pictures in short stories captured his lifelong love of writing poetry. In his lifetime Frank and poetry have become one. His ability to see, feel, and express experiences is as vivid and strong today as when he read those first short stories.

Jerry Treadway

(L-R) CHARLES JOHNSON, JERRY TREADWAY, AND FRANK BARONE